GET THE GIG

YUCK

by Matt and Dave

Join Yuck's fanclub at
YUCKWEB.COM

FOR MEGA
MAGICIANS:

Andrea   You   Pip

Faye   Jack Diego

Georgia   Alex

SIMON AND SCHUSTER

First published in Great Britain in 2009
by Simon & Schuster UK Ltd
A CBS COMPANY
1st Floor, 222 Gray's Inn Road, London WC1X 8HB

1 3 5 7 9 10 8 6 4 2

A CIP catalogue record for this book is
available from the British Library

ISBN 978-1-8473-8298-6

Printed and bound in Great Britain by
Cox & Wyman Ltd Reading Berkshire

www.simonsays.co.uk
www.yuckweb.com

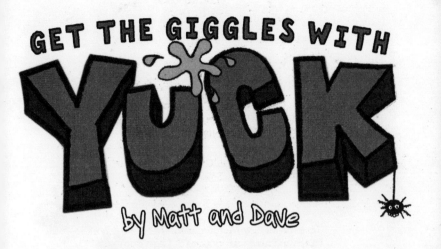

GET THE GIGGLES WITH

YUCK

by Matt and Dave

YUCK'S MEGA MAGIC WAND

AND

YUCK'S PIRATE TREASURE

Illustrated by Nigel Baines

YUCK'S MEGA MAGIC WAND

One evening, Yuck was in his bedroom trying on his new magician's costume from the fancy-dress shop.

He put on the black top hat and the black cape. Then he picked up the magician's wand and turned to face a frog that was sitting on his bed. "Fungus, we're going to be the stars of the show," he said.

"Ribbit," the frog croaked.

In two days' time, Yuck was going to be
performing magic at the school talent
show. Fungus the frog was going to be his
magician's assistant.

Yuck took off his top hat and the frog
hopped inside it, then he put the hat back
on and went downstairs to find Mum and
Dad. He wanted to practise his magic.

Dad was in the living room.

"Dad, do you want to see some magic?" Yuck asked.

"Can't you see I'm busy, Yuck?" Dad replied. He was watching television.

"But I'm Yucko the Incredible, the greatest magician in the world," Yuck said.

"Go on then, but make it quick."

"For my first trick, I shall need a handkerchief from the audience."

Dad took a white handkerchief from his pocket and handed it to Yuck.

"By the power of magic I shall make this handkerchief change colour," Yuck said. He tapped the handkerchief with his magic wand and said the magic word, "Alakazam!" He pointed to the window. "Quick, Dad, look over there!"

As Dad looked away, Yuck blew his nose into the handkerchief.

"See, it's changed colour!" Yuck said, handing it back.

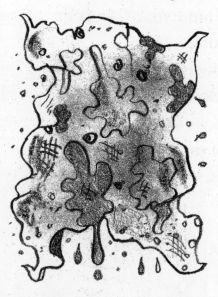

The handkerchief had changed from white to green. It was sticky and gooey and covered in snot.

"Yuck, that's not magic. That's revolting!" Dad said.

Yuck giggled, then ran to the kitchen to find Mum. She was sitting at the kitchen table sewing sequins onto a pink dress.

"Mum, do you want to see some magic?" he asked her.

"Yuck, can't you see I'm busy?" Mum replied.

"But I'm Yucko the Incredible, the greatest magician in the world," Yuck said.

"Go on then, but make it quick."

"For my next trick I'll need a coin from the audience."

From her pocket, Mum took a 20p coin and placed it on the table.

"By the power of magic I shall make this coin disappear," Yuck said. He tapped the coin with his wand, then said the magic word, "Alakazam!" He pointed to the window. "Quick, Mum, look over there!"

As Mum looked away, Yuck picked up the coin and slipped it into his pocket. "See, the coin's vanished!" he said.

Mum looked. "Very good, Yuck. Now give it back, please."

Yuck giggled. "I'm afraid I don't know how to make it reappear."

Just then, Yuck's sister, Polly Princess, stomped into the kitchen. "Mum, is my costume ready?" she asked.

"Yes, Polly," Mum told her. Mum held up the pink dress that she'd sewn with sequins. It was Polly's pop-star costume for the school talent show. The sequins spelled out the words: *Princess of Pop*.

"Shouldn't that say Princess of POOP?" Yuck asked, giggling.

Polly barged past him and grabbed the dress. She pulled it on over her T-shirt. "It's wonderful!" she said, twirling. "I'll be the star of the show!"

Polly started singing a song that she'd written for the talent show:

"I love school.
The teachers are great.
I love lessons.
I never arrive late…"

Mum clapped. "That was lovely, Polly."

"What a rubbish song," Yuck said. He had his fingers in his ears.

Polly scowled at Yuck. "You're just jealous because my act is better than yours."

"No it isn't," Yuck said. "I'm Yucko the Incredible, the greatest magician in the world."

"Then make a rabbit appear," Polly told him. "A real magician could make a fluffy white rabbit appear from his hat."

"If you insist," Yuck replied. He tapped his hat with his wand, then said the magic word, "Alakazam!" He took his hat off and held it out for Polly to see. "There you go."

"I don't see a rabbit," Polly said.

"Look inside," Yuck told her. He raised

the hat up to Polly's face. A long tongue flicked up and licked her chin.

"URGH!" Polly shrieked. "That's not a rabbit!" She was wiping frog spit from her face.

Yuck was giggling. "Oh, I thought you said 'ribbit'," he chuckled.

Fungus the frog hopped from the hat. "Ribbit," he croaked. "Ribbit, ribbit."

The frog hopped across the kitchen floor.

"Yuck, get that thing out of here!" Mum cried. "You're not allowed a frog in the house!"

"But Fungus is my assistant," Yuck said.

Fungus had followed Yuck into the house two days ago. He liked being with Yuck.

"I'll get rid of it," Polly said. She grabbed a dishcloth and threw it over the frog.

"Leave Fungus alone!" Yuck said.

Polly scooped up the frog and carried it to the back door. She threw Fungus outside.

"No!" Yuck said, rushing to save him.

Yuck looked out, but the garden was dark. Fungus was nowhere to be seen.

"Come on, both of you. It's time for bed," Mum said.

"But, Mum—"

Mum closed the back door. "Upstairs, now! You've got school in the morning."

Yuck and Polly headed out of the kitchen. Yuck was walking behind Polly, pointing his magic wand. "Alakazam! Alakazoo! Turn my sister into poo!"

Polly turned round. "You're useless at magic," she said. "You're going to get booed off the stage." She grabbed his magic wand and snapped it in two, then ran upstairs.

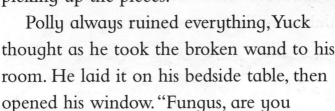

"My wand! You've broken it!" Yuck said, picking up the pieces.

Polly always ruined everything, Yuck thought as he took the broken wand to his room. He laid it on his bedside table, then opened his window. "Fungus, are you there?" he called.

"Ribbit!"

Fungus the Frog was hopping up the drainpipe. He hopped onto Yuck's window ledge.

"We'll get that nasty Polly back," Yuck said to him.

He placed Fungus on his pillow, then jumped into bed.

That night, Yuck dreamed that he and
Fungus were the stars of the world's biggest
talent show. In front of thousands of people
Yuck waved his magic wand. "Alakazam!"
Fungus the frog rose into the air, floating
above the audience. "Alakazam!" Fungus
grew to the size of an elephant.
"Alakazam!" He flicked out his massive
tongue, covering the audience in frog spit.

"Hooray!" the audience cheered.

The next morning, Yuck and Polly left for school. On the way they came to the fancy-dress shop. As Polly walked ahead, Yuck dashed inside to look for a new magic wand. He searched along the shelves, passing vampire costumes, spacemen costumes and clown costumes. But at the end of the aisle, where his magician's costume had been, the shelf was empty.

"Can I help you?" he heard.

Yuck turned and saw the old lady who owned the shop.

"Hello," Yuck said. "Where are the magicians' costumes?"

"I'm afraid you bought the last one yesterday," she told him.

"But my sister broke my wand," Yuck said. "I need a new one for the school talent show. I'm doing a magic act."

The lady went behind the counter and opened a drawer. "Would you be interested in a second-hand wand?" she asked, taking out a thin wooden case. She lifted the lid of the case and inside Yuck saw a black wand with silver ends. It was sparkling.

"Wow!" he said.

Engraved on its side were the words:
MEGA MAGIC WAND.

"I'm afraid it's rather old," the lady told him. "It once belonged to The Great Stupendo."

"The Great Stupendo?" Yuck asked.

"The Great Stupendo was a famous magician. I used to make his costumes."

"How much does the wand cost?" Yuck asked, feeling in his pockets. He only had the 20p coin that he'd got from Mum.

"Seeing as your other wand got broken, you can have this one for free," the lady said, smiling. She handed the Mega Magic Wand to Yuck.

"Thank you!" Yuck replied. He slipped the Mega Magic Wand into his pocket, then headed out of the door.

By the time Yuck arrived at school, the lesson had already begun. Mrs Wagon the Dragon was standing at the front of the class. "There's just one day left until the talent show," she announced. "Your parents will be coming to watch, and there will be an important visitor in the audience – Mr Disinfector, the school inspector!"

Yuck crawled along the floor trying to sneak to his desk.

"I'll be expecting you all to show the inspector how talented this school is."

The Dragon saw Yuck. "You're late!" she boomed, storming over and picking him up by his ankle.

"Sorry, Miss, I had to fetch something for my act."

"And what act might that be?"

"Magic, Miss," he said.

"Well it had better be good," the Dragon warned him. She hurled Yuck to the back of the class and he landed in his seat next to Little Eric.

Little Eric was reading a joke book.

"Why have you got that?" Yuck whispered to him.

"For my act. I'm going to tell jokes," Little Eric said.

"Right, you can all spend today practising for the show," the Dragon said.

Everyone in the class began practising. Schoolie Julie took some multicoloured balls from her bag and tried to juggle. Tall Paul tried to spin a basketball on his fingertip. Megan the Mouth put a trumpet to her lips and tried to play it. Frank the Tank tried to whistle. Ben Bong tried to do handstands. Fartin Martin and Tom Bum tried to break-dance.

While Yuck put on his magician's hat and cape, Little Eric told him a joke: "What do you get if you cross two elephants with a fish?"

"I don't know," Yuck said.

"Swimming trunks!" Little Eric said, laughing.

As Yuck laughed, his hat wobbled and Fungus the frog hopped out from underneath it.

"Cool, a frog!" Little Eric said.

Fungus hopped onto the desk and Yuck gave him a tickle. "Ribbit," Fungus croaked.

"Fungus is my assistant," Yuck explained.

Fungus hopped from the desk onto Frank the Tank's shoulder, then onto Megan the

Mouth's trumpet. He licked her nose.

"Urgh!" Megan the Mouth cried.

Yuck and Little Eric giggled as Fungus hopped from person to person, licking each with his long tongue.

"Urgh! It's a frog!" everyone cried.

The Dragon looked over. "A frog? Who's brought a frog to school?"

Yuck laughed as Fungus hopped onto the Dragon's desk and flicked out his long tongue, licking her glasses.

"Aaaaaargh!" she shrieked. "Get that out of here!"

Yuck ran to the front of the class and held out his hat. Fungus hopped inside it. "Don't worry, Miss. He's a friendly frog."

The Dragon grabbed Yuck by his ear. "Frogs are NOT allowed in school," she said. She dragged Yuck out of the classroom and up the corridor to Mr Reaper the headmaster's office.

The Reaper was sitting at his desk, clipping his nose hair.

"Mr Reaper, this disgusting boy has brought a frog to school," the Dragon said.

"Ribbit!" Fungus croaked from inside Yuck's hat.

"Leave this to me," the Reaper said. As the Dragon left, the Reaper opened his desk drawer and took out a glass jar. "Give that frog here," he said.

"But, Sir—"

"Give it to me!" the Reaper told him. He grabbed Fungus and popped him in the glass jar, then screwed the lid shut. "I shall get rid of it at lunchtime."

"But he's my friend," Yuck said.

The Reaper dragged Yuck out of his office and sat him on The Bench in the corridor. "Wait there while I think of a suitable punishment for you."

The Bench was where children sat when they were in BIG TROUBLE.

As the Reaper went back into his office, Yuck crept to the door. He peered in and saw Fungus in the jar on the Reaper's desk. Yuck had to save him. But how?

Just then, Yuck felt something tingle in his pocket. He looked down and saw the Mega Magic Wand lift out and rise into the air. It was sparkling.

Wow! Yuck thought. Magic!

The Mega Magic wand pressed itself into his hand and pointed through the door at the glass jar containing Fungus. "Alakazam!" Yuck said.

Suddenly, the wand let out a burst of
sparkles, and Fungus vanished from the jar.

Then Yuck heard a
"ribbit" as the frog
reappeared on his shoulder.

Fungus licked Yuck's ear and he smiled.

Yuck had an idea. He pointed the Mega
Magic Wand at the Reaper.
"Alakazam!"

The wand let out a burst of sparkles, and the Reaper vanished.

Then Yuck heard a cry from outside. "HEEEEEEELP!"

He ran off down the corridor. Children were hurrying from their classrooms to the playground. They were gathering around the school flagpole.

"HELP ME!" a voice cried.

Yuck looked up and saw the Reaper clinging to the top of the flagpole.

"GET ME DOWN!"

Everyone was laughing. The Dragon pushed her way to the front of the crowd. "Mr Reaper, what are you doing up there?" she called.

"I have no idea!" he shouted.

Yuck pointed the Mega Magic Wand.
"Alakazam," he said.

In a burst of sparkles, the Reaper's
trousers vanished. He was clinging to the
flagpole in his underpants! "What's
happening?" he shrieked.

Polly was in the crowd sniggering. The
Reaper's trousers reappeared on her head.
"Uurgh!" she cried.

"Polly, what are you doing
with my trousers?" the Reaper
shouted. He slid down the
flagpole getting splinters in
his bottom. "Ouch! Oo!
Argh!" He yanked the
trousers from Polly's head.
"Give those here!"

Yuck sneaked off
giggling with his
Mega Magic
Wand in his
pocket. This was
going to be fun!

That lunchtime, in the canteen, Yuck showed Little Eric the Mega Magic Wand.

"Wow!" Little Eric said, seeing it sparkle.

"Watch this," Yuck said, pointing it. He said the magic word, "Alakazam!"

In a burst of sparkles, food began rising from everyone's plates. Yuck and Little Eric giggled as sausages, beans, yoghurt and bananas floated into the air. Everyone stared upwards in astonishment.

Polly Princess was sitting with Juicy
Lucy. The food began collecting above
their heads like a cloud.

Yuck said the magic word, "Alakazam!"

Suddenly, the food dropped.

"UUUUUUUUURGH!" Polly and
Lucy shrieked,
as sausages,
beans, yoghurt
and bananas
splatted down
on them.

The Reaper
came running
in. He saw
Polly and Lucy covered in food. "Polly!
Lucy! What happened?"

"They were having a food fight, Sir,"
Yuck said.

"No we weren't," Polly cried. Beans were
dribbling down her cheek.

Yuck slipped the Mega Magic Wand into
his pocket, then sneaked off laughing.

That afternoon, everyone was in the assembly hall practising for the talent show.

Little Eric was trying to learn his jokes. "It's hard to remember them all," he told Yuck.

"Let me help you," Yuck said. He pointed the wand at Little Eric's joke book. "Alakazam!"

 In a burst of sparkles, the words rose off the pages and flew into Little Eric's ear. He began laughing and giggling, then started telling a joke: "What do you call a fish with no eyes?"

"I don't know," Yuck said.

"A fsh!"

Yuck laughed.

Little Eric's head was full of jokes! "Thanks, Yuck," he said.

Yuck saw Fartin Martin and Tom Bum trying to break-dance, but they kept falling over. "Do you want some help?" he asked.

"Yes please," they said.

Yuck pointed his Mega Magic Wand. "Alakazam!"

In a burst of sparkles, Fartin Martin started moonwalking. Tom Bum started doing Crazylegs. Then they both did The Robot.

"Wow!" they said. "How did you do that?"

"I am Yucko the Incredible, the greatest magician in the world!"

Yuck helped Schoolie Julie juggle six juggling balls at a time. He helped Tall Paul spin the basketball on his fingertip. He helped Ben Bong do a handstand.

The Mega Magic Wand was brilliant!

Yuck helped everyone practise their acts – everyone except Polly. She'd finished practising and was being a goodie goodie, painting a banner that said **SCHOOL TALENT SHOW**. She was on the stage at the end of the hall, standing on a ladder with a paintbrush and a tin of red paint.

Yuck pointed the wand. "Alakazam!"

Suddenly the ladder vanished beneath her, and Polly fell to the ground, landing on her bottom and splashing paint all over herself.

The Dragon came in and saw the red paint everywhere. "Polly, what happened?" she asked.

"The ladder vanished!" Polly said.

"Vanished?"

Yuck pointed the wand. "Alakazam!"

Polly jumped up
and her paintbrush
began painting the
Dragon's face.

"Stop that, you stupid
girl," the Dragon shrieked.

Polly tried to stop the
paintbrush, but it was out of control! It
painted the Dragon's hair then up and
down her body.

The Reaper came running in. "What's
going on?" he yelled.

Yuck pointed his Mega
Magic Wand. "Alakazam!"

Suddenly, the Reaper's
shoes turned into banana
skins. He skidded into Polly
and the Dragon, knocking them both over.

All three were sliding around the floor,
covered in paint. Everyone in the school
was laughing.

Yuck slipped the Mega Magic Wand in
his pocket, then sneaked off giggling.

That evening, at home, Yuck tried out his yucky magic, practising for the talent show. He placed his hat upside down on the floor and tapped it with the Mega Magic Wand. "Alakazam!"

There was a gurgling sound as slime started bubbling from the hat. Then, with a **WHOOSH**, out shot a fountain of snot, scabs and toenail clippings. Underpants flew out, and a smelly sock. Fungus the frog hopped from the hat, doing a somersault.

"Brilliant!" Yuck said.

"Ribbit," Fungus croaked. The bedroom door burst open and Fungus dived under the bed.

It was Polly. She saw the hat bubbling over with slime. Then she saw the Mega Magic Wand in Yuck's hand. It was sparkling.

"It was YOU!" she said. "YOU made those things happen today! That wand really IS magic!"

"Go away, Polly," Yuck said.

"Give it to me!" Polly told him, reaching for the wand.

"No way."

"Mum!" Polly called. "Come and see what Yuck's been doing!"

Mum came running upstairs to Yuck's room. She saw the mess everywhere.

"What on earth's been going on in here, Yuck?" she asked.

"Nothing," Yuck told her.

Mum heard a "ribbit!" from under Yuck's bed. A long tongue flicked out and licked her ankle. "Urgh! It's that frog! I told you: no frogs in the house!"

"Get rid of it, Mum," Polly said. "Throw it outside!"

Mum picked Fungus up. "Now clean your room, Yuck," she said, and she carried Fungus downstairs.

"That was mean, Polly," Yuck said. "Fungus likes staying with me."

Polly sniggered. "Serves you right for not giving me that wand." She stuck out her tongue, then ran downstairs to find Mum.

Yuck decided that when he was EMPEROR OF EVERYTHING, he'd live in a magic palace full of frogs. Polly would live outside in the cold. He'd turn her legs into frogs' legs and make her hop up and down in a stinky pond.

Yuck looked out of his window and saw
Mum place Fungus in the middle of lawn.
As she went back inside, he pointed his
wand. "Alakazam!"

In a burst of sparkles, Fungus reappeared
on Yuck's bed. Yuck gave him a tickle.

"Ribbit," Fungus croaked.

"Don't worry. Tomorrow we'll show
them," Yuck said. "Our act is going to be
the best." He placed his hat and cape by his
bed, and laid his Mega Magic Wand on top
ready for the next day.

In the morning, Yuck woke up excited. But when he went to put his costume on, he found that his Mega Magic Wand was missing! Yuck rushed downstairs. "Polly!" he called. "Polly, what have you done with it?"

"Polly's already left for school," Mum told him.

Yuck quickly popped Fungus under his hat and ran to school. He found Polly practising her act in the assembly hall. She was wearing her pink dress with sequins and singing her song.

"You've stolen my Mega Magic Wand, haven't you?" Yuck said to her.

"I don't know what you're talking about," Polly said, grinning.

Yuck saw the wand poking out of her pocket. "Yes you do. Give it back!"

Polly pulled out the wand and pointed it at him. "Keep away or I'll turn you into a slug!"

Yuck leapt on Polly, wrestling her to the ground. But just as he was about to grab the wand, the Dragon came in.

"Yuck, no fighting!" the Dragon yelled, pulling him off.

"He's trying to stop me practising for the show, Miss," Polly gasped. "He doesn't want anyone to be better than him."

"Spoiling other people's acts is NOT allowed, Yuck!" the Dragon said, dragging him away.

"But, Miss—"

"For your punishment, you are officially BANNED from the talent show!"

That lunchtime, everyone's parents arrived, including Yuck's mum and dad. They sat in the assembly hall, waiting for the talent show to begin. Two red curtains were pulled across the stage and all the performers stood at the side, ready to take their turn.

Yuck had to sit with the grown-ups. He still had his magician's costume on, with Fungus hidden under his hat, but he wasn't allowed to perform. The Dragon sat beside him, and on his other side was Mr Disinfector, the school inspector.

"What's your name, boy?" Mr Disinfector asked.

"Yuck," Yuck said.

"And why aren't you in the show?"

"Because I'm not allowed."

The Reaper stepped from behind the curtains onto the stage. "It gives me great pleasure to welcome you all to the school talent show. If you're sitting comfortably, then we'll begin!"

He stood aside as the curtains opened.

Little Eric was the first to perform. "For my act I'd like to tell some jokes," he said. "What do you get if…" Little Eric paused. "Why did the…" He scratched his head. "Knock…"

Something's wrong, Yuck thought.

Little Eric couldn't get his words out.

Yuck looked over and saw Polly Princess at the side of the stage pointing the Mega Magic Wand. She was casting a spell on Little Eric, making him forget his jokes.

"Boooo! Get off!" Polly called.

Little Eric blushed with embarrassment. Quickly, he ran off the stage.

"He wasn't very good," Mr Disinfector said to Yuck.

Little Eric's mum and dad were the only people clapping.

"It wasn't his fault," Yuck said. "It was my sister, Polly. She ruined his act!"

At the side of the stage, Polly was giggling.

Next to perform were Fartin Martin and Tom Bum. But when they tried to break-dance, their legs wobbled like jelly. They fell over, rolling off the stage.

Yuck saw Polly pointing the Mega
Magic wand at them.

"Boooo! You're hopeless," she shouted.

Yuck stood up. "It's not their fault," he
called. "Polly's ruining their act!"

"Sit down, Yuck," the Dragon said,
pulling him back onto his seat.

"But, Miss, Polly's doing magic on them!"

"Don't be ridiculous," the Dragon told
him. "Now be quiet and watch the rest of
the show."

Next up was Schoolie Julie. She tried to juggle, but the balls stuck to her hands.

When Tall Paul tried to spin his basketball, it burst.

When Frank the Tank

tried to whistle, he couldn't move his lips.

When Megan the Mouth tried to play her trumpet,

it went all floppy. One by one, Polly ruined everyone's act – even Juicy Lucy's.

When Lucy tried to spin a hula-hoop around her waist, it shot off into the audience.

Soon only Polly was left to perform. She stepped onto the stage in her sparkling pink dress. "I'm going to sing a song," she announced. "It's called 'I love school'."

Yuck had to do something. He tapped the Dragon on the shoulder.

"What is it?" she asked.

"Look over there," he said, pointing to the window. As the Dragon looked away, Yuck dived down and crawled under the chair in front. He pushed between the parents' legs heading for the stage, then hid behind the curtain at its side. He could see

the Mega Magic Wand poking from Polly's dress pocket. Yuck reached out and grabbed it. From behind the curtain, he pointed it at her. "Alakazam!"

I hate school the teachers are SMELLY

Princess of Pop

Polly started to sing:
"I hate school.
The teachers
are SMELLY."
Yuck heard parents
in the audience tutting.
The Mega Magic
Wand was changing
her words.

"Lessons are boring.
I'd rather watch telly."

"Polly, how DARE you!" the Reaper
shouted. He stood up in the front row.
He was fuming.

"But, Sir," Polly
said. "I—"
Yuck pointed
the wand again.
"Alakazam!"

Polly stuck her tongue out at the Reaper.
The audience gasped. They watched as
her tongue grew longer and longer, and
licked the Reaper's face.

50

"Urgh!" the Reaper cried.

"Ribbit," Polly croaked. Then all of a sudden, she vanished.

Mum stood up in the audience. "What on earth's going on?"

Dad stood up. "Where did our daughter go?"

Behind the curtain, Yuck pointed his
Mega Magic Wand at the other children.

"Alakazam!"

In a burst of
sparkles, Schoolie
Julie appeared
on the stage.
She was juggling
ten balls – with
one hand!

"Alakazam!"
Tall Paul
appeared on the
stage spinning
his basketball –
on his nose!

"Alakazam!"
Megan the
Mouth appeared
playing her
trumpet – with
her ear!

"Alakazam!" Fartin Martin and Tom Bum appeared on the stage break-dancing – spinning on their heads!

"Alakazam!" Little Eric appeared on the stage giggling. "Why did the dog sit next to the fire?" he called.

"We don't know," the audience said.

"Because he wanted to be a hot dog!"

The audience laughed. They started clapping. The stage was soon full of all the children doing their acts. And they were ALL brilliant!

Mr Disinfector stood up. "How amazing!" he said. "What talented children!"

"It's magic!" everyone said.

"Magic?" the inspector asked.

Yuck stepped out onto the stage with his Mega Magic Wand. "I'm glad you like the show," he said. "I'm Yucko the Incredible, the greatest magician in the world!"

Yuck lifted his hat, and Fungus the frog hopped up and down on his head – doing somersaults!

"A somersaulting frog!" Mr Disinfector said. "I've never seen anything so marvellous! I declare Yuck and his frog the stars of the show!"

"But that's not fair!" a voice called. It was a tiny croaky voice and it came from underneath the inspector's chair.

Mr Disinfector bent down and saw a second frog hopping by his foot. He picked it up. It was dressed in a tiny pink dress with sequins spelling out the words Princess of Pop. The frog hopped up and down on his hand.

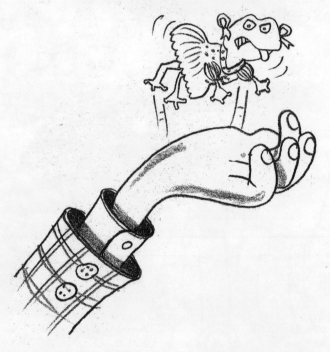

Mum looked over. "Polly," she cried. "Is that you?"

Dad looked over. "Polly, what on earth's happened to you?'

Polly was slimy and green. She flicked out her tongue. "Ribbit!" she said. "I hate you, Yuck! Ribbit!"

Yuck was on the stage, laughing. "Now THAT'S what I call magic!"

YUCK'S PIRATE TREASURE

"Land ahoy, me hearties!" Yuck said.

Yuck's sister Polly Princess turned round from the front seat of the car. "Yuck, stop talking like that. You're getting on my nerves."

Yuck was in the back seat. He was wearing a skull-and-crossbones hat and had an eye patch over one eye. "But I'm a pirate. That's how pirates talk," he told her.

"You're not a pirate," Polly said, reaching back and pinging the elastic eye patch so it hit Yuck's face.

"OUCH!" he said.

"Can you two please behave?" Mum said from the driver's seat. She was driving Yuck and Polly to the seaside for the day.

Little Eric and Juicy Lucy were coming too. Little Eric was sitting in the back beside Yuck. He wore an eye patch over his glasses and had drawn a beard on his face in felt-tip pen.

"Hoist the main sail!" Yuck said to him.

"Shiver me timbers!" Little Eric replied.

"Pieces of eight!"

"Yo ho ho!"

"STOP TALKING LIKE THAT!" Polly screamed.

Polly reached back and snatched Yuck's pirate hat.

"Hey, give that back!" Yuck said. He picked his nose and wiped a bogey on Polly's hair.

"Urrrgh!" she cried.

Yuck grabbed his hat back. "Don't mess with pirates!" he warned her. "You'll never win."

"Behave, both of you!" Mum told them.

While Polly scraped the bogey from her hair, Yuck looked out of the window. "Are we nearly there yet?" he asked.

"Just a few more minutes," Mum said.

Yuck couldn't wait to get to the seaside. They were heading to Buccaneer Cove, the home of Pirate Pete. In the Pirate Pete play area there was a tall pirate ship with climbing ropes and a telescope.

"Here we are!" Mum said, pulling up in the car park by the beach.

Everybody got out. From the boot of the car, Mum took her beach bag, a picnic box and a bundle of towels. Polly and Lucy took out two pink buckets and spades.

"Did you bring your bucket and spade, Yuck?" Mum asked.

"Pirates don't need buckets and spades," Yuck told her.

Yuck and Little Eric reached into the boot of the car and took out two plastic pirate swords. They clashed them together, pretending to have a sword fight.

"Arrgh," Yuck said, falling to the ground.

Yuck opened one eye and looked over to the Pirate Pete play area. On the deck of the ship, standing at the wheel, was a life-sized statue of Pirate Pete. It had an eye patch, a black beard and a wooden leg. Next to the ship was the Pirate Pete café where children were queuing up for ice cream.

"Can we have an ice cream please, Mum?" Yuck asked.

"No, Yuck," Mum said.

"But pirates LOVE ice cream," he told her.

"Then you shouldn't have been naughty in the car."

Yuck glared at Polly. It was all her fault.

Yuck decided that when he was
EMPEROR OF EVERYTHING, he would
sail away in a pirate ship full of ice cream.
If Polly tried to climb aboard, he'd tie her
up and make her walk the plank into
shark-infested waters.

Everyone followed Mum onto the beach, where she laid a towel on the sand to sunbathe. "I want you all to play nicely today," she said.

"Lucy and I are going to collect shells," Polly told her.

"Boring!" Yuck said. "Little Eric and I are going to play pirates!" They ran off to the Pirate Pete play area, waving their plastic swords.

They jumped onto the pirate ship and climbed up to the top of the mast.

"All aboard!" Little Eric called.

"Prepare to set sail!" Yuck said.

They slid down again, and Little Eric stood beside Pirate Pete's statue, taking hold of the ship's wheel.

Yuck stood at the ship's telescope, peering through it. He saw Mum sunbathing, and Polly and Lucy looking for shells. He had an idea. "Polly!" he called.

Polly looked over. "What do you want?" she called back.

"Come here, I've got something to show you!"

Polly walked across the beach with her bucket and spade. She clambered onto the deck of the pirate ship. "It had better be good," she said.

"Oh, it is," Yuck said. He ran to the side of the ship where a long plank stuck out over the sand. "Come over here," he told her.

Polly stepped over. "What is it?"

"Just a bit further and you'll see."

As Polly approached the plank, Yuck pressed his plastic sword to her back. "Got you!" he said.

Little Eric stepped forward with his sword. They had her surrounded.

"Let me go!" she said.

Yuck smiled. "Walk the plank, you slimy sea-slug!" He marched Polly along the plank, and she tumbled off its end.

"Aaargh!" she cried, landing face first in the sand. She sat up, spitting. There was sand in her mouth and sand in her hair. Lucy came over to help her up.

"I hate you, Yuck!" Polly said.

"That's for getting us into trouble in the car," Yuck told her. "I warned you not to mess with pirates."

"Are you okay?" a man called.

Yuck looked round. Outside the Pirate Pete café he saw the owner looking at them. "We're just playing pirates," Yuck told him.

Little Eric stood by the statue of Pirate Pete and held up his sword. "Pirate Pete's the best," he called.

"No he's not, he's stupid!" Polly said, picking up her bucket and spade.

The café owner stepped over. "I wouldn't say bad things about Pirate Pete if I were you," he said to her. "His ghost might hear you."

"His ghost?" Polly asked.

"Pirate Pete visited these shores hundreds of years ago," the café owner explained.

"They say that his ghost still haunts the beach, guarding his treasure."

"Treasure?" Yuck asked excitedly. He leapt down from the ship.

"They say he hid a treasure chest somewhere round here – full of gold coins!"

"What a load of rubbish," Polly muttered.

"Pirates not your thing, eh?" the café owner asked her. He looked at Polly's bucket and spade. "Maybe you'd prefer this?" he said, unrolling a long piece of paper. It was a poster. He stuck it to a railing outside the café. "There's a sandcastle competition today."

"Brilliant! Sandcastles!" Polly said. "What's the prize?"

"A Super-Dooper Multi-Scoop ice cream," the café owner told her. He smiled then went back into the café.

"I love ice cream!" Lucy said. "Yummy!"

Polly turned to Yuck and stuck her tongue out. "I bet you wish you'd brought a bucket and spade now. We're going to win that ice cream."

She ran off with Lucy, giggling.

Little Eric turned to Yuck. "That's not fair," he said. "I'd love to win an ice cream."

Yuck was still thinking about what the café owner had said. "Don't worry, we don't need to build a sandcastle," he said. "Soon we'll be able to buy all the ice cream in the world."

"How?" Little Eric asked.

Yuck smiled. "We're going to find Pirate Pete's treasure," he said. "And when we do we'll be rich!"

Yuck and Little Eric ran off across the the beach and went exploring.

They ran past children building sandcastles, to the side of the beach where there were caves.

"What if Pirate Pete hid it in a cave?" Little Eric asked.

Yuck stepped into the entrance of a big cave. It was dark and spooky. He imagined Pirate Pete, hundreds of years ago, dragging his treasure chest inside.

Little Eric stepped in nervously. "But what if his ghost is in here?"

"Pirate Pete's ghost won't harm us," Yuck said. He lifted his eye patch. "We're pirates too, remember!"

Yuck crept to the back of the cave and saw a plastic orange crate with barnacles stuck to its side. It looked old.

"A treasure chest!" Little Eric said, excitedly.

Yuck looked inside the crate, but it was just an old fishing crate that had been washed in by the waves. It was full of seaweed and crabs.

"I know what we can do with this," Yuck said. He picked a crab from the crate and carried it outside to the beach. Quietly, he crept up behind Polly as she was building her sandcastle. He placed the crab by her foot.

"OUCH!" Polly cried, leaping up.

The crab was pinching her toe with its claw.

Yuck and Little Eric giggled as she hopped across the sand, shrieking. "OO! EEE! OOOW!"

Her foot plunged right through a
sandcastle that a small boy was building.
"Hey, mind my
sandcastle!" the boy cried.

The boy's dad came running over.
"What's going on?" he asked.

"That nasty girl jumped on my
sandcastle!" the boy said, pointing at Polly.

Polly pulled the crab from her toe. "It
wasn't my fault," she said.

Mum came running over. "Polly, what
have you done?"

"She's ruined my sandcastle," the little
boy said.

"Polly, say sorry," Mum told her.

"But it was an accident," Polly cried.

"What a horrible girl," the boy's dad said, leading the boy away. "Come on, I'll buy you an ice cream on the way home."

Mum frowned at Polly. "Polly, from now on, play nicely!" she said. Then she went back to her towel to sunbathe.

Polly looked at Yuck. "It was you, wasn't it? YOU put that crab there!"

Yuck giggled and ran off with Little Eric to look for Pirate Pete's treasure.

"What if his treasure chest got smashed on the rocks in a storm?" Little Eric said.

Yuck and Little Eric looked among the rocks and rock pools by the water's edge, searching for gold coins.

"Look at this!" Little Eric said, pointing at one of the pools. The tip of a tentacle was poking from it. Little Eric touched the tentacle and it coiled around his finger.

"Wow!" Yuck said. "An octopus!"

Yuck had an idea. He called across the beach: "Polly, come and look at this."

"What is it now?" Polly yelled.

"I've found a pretty shell that would look lovely on your sandcastle," Yuck called back.

"You'd better not be lying," Polly said, stomping over.

"It's in there," Yuck said, pointing to the rock pool.

Polly looked into the water. "I can't see a shell," she said.

"It's at the bottom," Little Eric told her.

Polly leaned down to get a closer look.

Just then, the tentacle reached up and coiled around her ear. "Aaarrrggghhh!" she screamed. Another tentacle reached up and coiled around her neck. "Uuurrrggghhh!"

Six more tentacles reached out of the rock pool, wrapping around her head, gripping like a mask. She turned and staggered across the beach, trying to pull the octopus from her face. "HELP!"

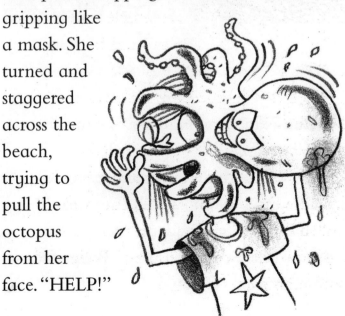

Polly couldn't see where she was going.
She trod on a sandcastle that a little girl
was building.

"Hey, mind my sandcastle!" the girl
shouted.

Mum came running over. "Polly, what
have you done?"

She saw the little girl's sandcastle
trampled in the sand. "Polly, say sorry!"

"But it was an accident," Polly cried.
Lucy pulled the octopus from Polly's face
and it crawled off down the beach.

"You're mean!" the little girl said.

The girl's mum led her away. "Don't worry, darling. I'll buy you an ice cream on the way home."

Mum frowned at Polly. "I told you to play nicely!" she said.

She dragged Polly up the beach, and Lucy followed them. Yuck and Little Eric were giggling.

"Come on," Mum called to them. "It's time for lunch."

Everyone sat around the picnic box.
"Now, who would like a salad sandwich?"
Mum asked, pulling out a stack of
sandwiches and paper plates.

"Urgh," Yuck said. "Haven't you got any
ketchup sandwiches instead?"

"Salad is good for you, Yuck," Mum
replied, handing a sandwich to each of them.

While Mum wasn't looking, Yuck buried
his in the sand. "I've finished," he said.

"That was quick, Yuck," Mum said.

"Can I have an ice cream now?"

"Don't let him," Polly told her. "He's
been naughty all morning."

"Yuck, I told you before, you're not
having one," Mum said.

Polly stuck her tongue out at Yuck. "And
you're not getting any of ours when we
win the competition," she sniggered. Polly

and Lucy looked over at
their sandcastle. It was a
tall, fairy sandcastle
with towers and a moat.

While Polly had her back turned, Yuck quickly sneaked her sandwich from her plate and filled it with sand. Then he put it back, giggling.

Polly picked it up. She bit into it. "Uuurrggghhh!" she cried, spitting. "My sandwich is full of sand!"

She threw it away, then stood up and scowled at Yuck. "I hate you, Yuck!" she said. She stormed off down the beach and Lucy ran after her.

"Hey, where do you two think you're going?" Mum called after them.

"To finish our sandcastle," Polly called back. "We're going to win an ice cream!"

Yuck was laughing. He watched as a
seagull flew down and gobbled the remains
of Polly's sandwich. It
took off again and flew
to the railing beside the
café. Yuck saw dozens
of seagulls perched in a
line. He stood up. "Can
we go and play now,
Mum?" he asked.

"Go on then," Mum said. "But be good."

Yuck ran off with Little Eric. They
headed to the railing with the seagulls
perched on it. The railing was covered with
white dollops of seagull poop. At one end
was a rubbish bin. Yuck reached into the
bin and took out a soggy
old ice cream cone. "Let's
make Polly an
ice cream she'll
never forget,"
he said to
Little Eric.

They walked along the railing scraping off seagull poop and putting it into the cone. They scooped up dollop after dollop until the cone was piled high like an ice cream.

Yuck carried it down the beach.

"Hey, Polly," he said. "How's your sandcastle coming along?"

Polly saw the ice cream in Yuck's hand. "Where did you get that from?" she asked.

"The café owner gave it to me," Yuck told her. "It's a Super-Dooper Pooper Scoop!"

"That's not fair! Give me some!"

Polly snatched it from him, and Yuck watched as she took a big lick from the mound of bird poop.

"UUURRRGGGHHH!" she screamed.

"What's the matter, Polly? Don't you like it?" Yuck asked.

Bird poop was smeared round Polly's lips. Her face turned green.

BLURGH!

She spewed up all over a sandcastle that two little boys were building.

"Hey, mind where you're puking!" the boys shouted.

Beside them on the sand was a plastic dinghy. Polly spewed up on that too.

The boys' dad came running over. "What's going on?" he asked.

"That girl just sicked up on our sandcastle!" one boy said, pointing at Polly.

"And on our dinghy!" the other said.

Polly was wiping the sick and seagull poop from her mouth.

Mum came running over. "Polly, are you okay?" she asked. She saw the boys' sandcastle and dinghy covered in sick.

"She's gross!" the boys said.

Their dad led them away. "Come on, you two, I'll buy you each an ice cream on the way home."

"But what about our dinghy?"

"Leave it. It's covered in sick. I'll buy you a new one."

Mum frowned at Polly. "Whatever's the matter with you today?" she asked.

"It wasn't my fault!" Polly said.

"She's trying to ruin the other sandcastles so she wins the competition," Yuck told Mum.

"No I'm not!" Polly said.

"Polly, that's terrible." Mum took away Polly's bucket and spade. "If you can't play nicely, you can't play at all."

"But Mum—"

"You too, Lucy," Mum said, taking her bucket and spade. "You'll BOTH have to find something else to do."

She led Polly and Lucy off up the beach.

Yuck and Little Eric were giggling. They looked at the plastic dinghy that the boys had left.

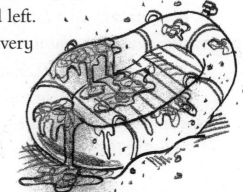

"It can be our very own pirate ship," Little Eric said.

"Let's launch it!" Yuck said.

They dragged the dinghy down the
beach and washed the sick off in the sea.
Then they jumped in and started paddling.

Polly and Lucy came running to find
them. "Hey, give us a go!" they called.

Polly and Lucy splashed into the sea and
swam after Yuck and Little Eric.

"Go away! It's our pirate ship," Yuck said.

Polly and Lucy reached onto the sides of
the dinghy and started climbing in.

"It's OURS now!" Polly grinned.

"Abandon ship!" Yuck said.

Quickly, Yuck and Little Eric jumped from the dinghy, then Yuck reached up and pulled out the air valve. The air came whizzing out of the dinghy as it shot across the water towards the beach.

"HEEEEELP!" Polly and Lucy screamed.

Polly and Lucy whizzed over the waves and onto the sand, flattening three more sandcastles.

"Hey, mind where you're going!" three children shouted.

Their parents came running over. "What's happened?" they asked.

"Those girls ruined our sandcastles!" the children said, pointing at Polly and Lucy.

"It wasn't our fault," Polly and Lucy said, climbing out of the deflated dinghy.

Mum rushed over and saw the flattened sandcastles. "Polly, Lucy, look what you've done! Say sorry!"

"But it was an accident," Polly said.

"You're nasty girls," the children said.

Their parents led them away. "Come on
now. Never mind the competition. We'll buy
you each an ice cream on the way home."

Yuck came strolling up the beach. "Have
Polly and Lucy been ruining the other
sandcastles again, Mum?"

Mum looked
around the
beach. Only
Polly and
Lucy's fairy
sandcastle was
still standing.

"Polly, Lucy, I'm shocked at you!" she
said. "Go and tell the man at the café what
you've done. You don't deserve to win that
competition. You should be disqualified."

"But, Mum—"

"No buts, Polly. Go and tell him this instant!"

Yuck and Little Eric giggled as Polly and Lucy trudged off up the beach to the café.

"I don't see why we should apologise," Lucy said. "It was all Yuck's fault."

"We're not going to," Polly whispered, sniggering. They walked up to the counter of the Pirate Pete café.

"Can we have our prize now, please?" Polly asked the café owner. She pointed down the beach to their fairy sandcastle.

"I'm afraid judging isn't until three o'clock," the café owner said. "There's still an hour to go."

"But there aren't any other sandcastles on the beach," Polly told him. "We're the winners."

"Someone might still want to build one," the café owner told her.

Polly stormed off crossly. As she passed the competition poster she tore it down and stuffed it into the rubbish bin.

"No one else is going to build a sandcastle now," she giggled.

Lucy smiled, and they hurried back down the beach to their fairy sandcastle.

Yuck and Little Eric were rolling on the sand laughing. "What, no ice cream? Polly and Lucy built a big sandcastle for nothing!"

"No we didn't," Polly told them. "We're still going to win, and when we do, we'll have a Super-Dooper Multi-Scoop ice cream. And you won't have any!"

Yuck and Little Eric stood up.

"Weren't you disqualified?" Little Eric asked.

"No, we weren't," Juicy Lucy told him.

Yuck glanced at the fairy sandcastle. "Well, it doesn't bother us," he said. "Soon Little Eric and I will be able to buy all the ice cream in the world!"

"How?" Polly asked.

"We're going to find Pirate Pete's treasure."

"Don't be stupid. There is no treasure," Polly said.

"Oh yes there is," Yuck told her. "And we've found a treasure map to prove it."

Yuck smiled then strolled off with Little Eric following.

"What treasure map?" Little Eric asked.

"I'll show you," Yuck whispered. "I've got a plan." He ran to Mum. "Have you got a pen and paper, please?" he asked her.

Mum was sunbathing. She opened her eyes and raised her sunglasses. "What for, Yuck?"

"It's pretty here. I thought I'd do some drawing," Yuck said.

Mum took a pen and paper from her bag and handed them to Yuck.

As she lay back down to sunbathe, he began drawing a treasure map. Quietly, he picked up the buckets and  spades that Mum had confiscated from Polly and Lucy, then sneaked off across the beach with Little Eric.

Polly and Lucy came running to find them. "Hey! What are you doing with our buckets and spades? Hands off!"

"We're going to dig for treasure," Yuck said. He showed Polly and Lucy his treasure map. Scrawled on it were the words PROPERTY OF PIRATE PETE. It looked like a map of the beach.

"Wow! Where did you get that?" Juicy Lucy asked.

"We found it in that cave," Yuck told them, pointing across the beach. "The problem is, we don't understand what this X means."

In the centre of the map was a big X.

"That's easy," Lucy said. "The X is where the—'

Polly nudged Lucy in the ribs. "It's probably just a smudge," she said.

"No, it's where the—'

"Lucy, it's probably nothing," Polly said, winking at her.

"It's such a shame," Yuck said to Little Eric. "It would have been great to have found all that gold. We would have been rich!"

Yuck screwed up the map and dropped it on the sand. He handed Polly her bucket and spade. "Here you are, Polly. I guess you might as well have these back."

Little Eric handed his bucket and spade to Lucy. "Come on, Yuck," he said. "Let's go and play."

Yuck and Little Eric headed off down the beach.

"Do you think they fell for it?" Little Eric whispered.

Yuck glanced over his shoulder. Polly had picked up the treasure map and was looking at it. "I think so," he giggled.

Yuck and Little Eric hid in the big cave and watched as Polly and Lucy examined the map.

"The X is where the treasure is," Lucy said.

"I know," Polly replied. "But I wasn't going to tell THEM that."

The map had waves marking the sea. There were caves and rock pools drawn at one edge, and a dotted line that ran from them to the big X in the middle. Along the dotted line were the words WALK 13 PACES.

Polly and Lucy ran to the rock pools then paced across the beach counting their footsteps. "One… two… three… four… five… six… seven… eight… nine… ten… eleven… twelve…" They stopped. They were standing in front of their fairy sandcastle.

"Oh no," Polly said. She looked again at the map. "Pirate Pete's treasure is buried underneath our sandcastle!"

"What about the competition?" Lucy asked.

Polly thought for a second. "What do you want: a Super-Dooper Multi-Scoop ice cream or all the ice cream in the world?"

"All the ice cream in the world!"

Polly and Lucy dug their spades into their fairy sandcastle. They dug out spadeful after

spadeful of sand, throwing it over their shoulders. Soon the fairy sandcastle was ruined. In its place was a huge hole, with a mound of sand piled up beside it.

Yuck and Little Eric watched, giggling, as Polly and Lucy dug deeper and deeper, throwing sand up out of the hole. The mound beside them grew bigger and bigger.

Quickly, Yuck fetched the orange crate
from the back of the cave and handed it to
Little Eric. "Meet me behind that mound of
sand," he said. Then he ran to where Mum
was sunbathing. Her eyes were closed.
Quietly, he took a white towel from beside
her then raced back to find Little Eric.

They hid behind the mound of sand beside the hole.

Yuck put the white towel over his head then stepped out and peered down at Polly and Lucy. "Woo-ooo-ooo," he called.

Polly and Lucy stopped digging and looked up from the bottom of the hole.

"Woo-ooo-ooo," Yuck said again.

"What's that?" Polly whispered.

Lucy held tightly to Polly. "It's a g-g-ghost!" she stuttered nervously.

"I am the ghost of Pirate Pete, and I've come to get you!" Yuck said.

"Don't hurt us!" Polly pleaded.

"Then repeat after me: 'Pirates are the best'."

Polly and Lucy were trembling. They looked up at the ghost. "P-pirates are the b-best," they said, frightened.

Keeping the towel over his head, Yuck picked up the orange crate. "Are you after my treasure?"

Polly stared at the crate. "W-we were j-just l-l-looking for it."

"Well, seeing as you think pirates are the best, I'll let you have it," Yuck said. He placed the crate at the edge of the hole. "Woo-oo-ooo. Help yourselves."

He stepped back and hid behind the mound of sand with Little Eric. They watched as Polly's hand reached up from the hole and grabbed the side of the crate. She pulled it towards her and it toppled over.

"AARRRGGGGHHHHHHH!"

Yuck and Little Eric peered over the edge of the hole.

Polly and Lucy were covered in seaweed. Dozens of crabs were nipping at their ears and pinching their toes. "OUCH! OOH! ARGH!" they screamed. "GET US OUT OF HERE!"

Mum came running over. "What's going on?"

She looked down into the hole.

"It was Pirate Pete's ghost!" Lucy screamed, pulling a crab from her ear.

Polly saw Yuck holding the white towel. "It was Yuck!" she yelled. "He tricked us!"

Just then, the café owner came walking down the beach carrying the biggest ice cream Yuck had ever seen: a Super-Dooper

Multi-Scoop! "Are there any entrants for the sandcastle competition?" the café owner asked.

"I'm afraid not," Mum said to him. "All the sandcastles are ruined."

Mum was helping Polly and Lucy get out of the hole.

"Oh what a shame," the café owner said. "It's three o'clock. What am I going to do with this prize?"

"Not EVERY sandcastle is ruined," Yuck said to the café owner. He stepped over to the big mound of sand that Polly and Lucy had thrown up from the hole, then took off his pirate hat and placed it on the top. "This big sandcastle is mine and Little Eric's," he said.

"It's a pirate sandcastle."

"Hey, that's not fair!" Polly yelled,
shaking crabs from her hair.

Yuck and Little Eric smiled as the cafe
owner handed them the Super-Dooper
Multi-Scoop ice cream. "Congratulations,"
he said to them. "I declare the pirates
the winners!"

Yuck and Little Eric both took a big lick of the ice cream. It tasted of chocolate and strawberry and butterscotch and mint and banana and raspberry and marshmallow.

"Yo ho ho!" they said. "Pirates LOVE ice cream!"

GET THE GIGGLES WITH ALL YUCK'S BOOKS!

YUCK'S SLIME MONSTER
(and Yuck's Gross Party)

YUCK'S AMAZING UNDERPANTS
(and Yuck's Scary Spider)

YUCK'S PET WORM
(and Yuck's Rotten Joke)

YUCK'S MEGA MAGIC WAND
(and Yuck's Pirate Treasure)

YUCK'S FART CLUB
(and Yuck's Sick Trick)

YUCK'S ALIEN ADVENTURE
(and Yuck's Slobbery Dog)

YUCK'S ABOMINABLE BURP BLASTER
(and Yuck's Remote Control Revenge)

YUCK'S BIG BOGEYS
(and Yuck's Smelly Socks)

YUCK'S SUPERCOOL SNOTMAN
(and Yuck's Dream Machine)

Join Yuck's fanclub at
YUCKWEB.COM